P
SPI

D0605702

YUBA COUNTY LIBRARY
MARYSVILLE

City Angel

by Eileen Spinelli illustrations by Kyrsten Brooker

Dial Books for Young Readers New York

Published by Dial Books for Young Readers ✳ A division of Penguin Young Readers Group ✳ 345 Hudson Street, New York, New York, 10014 ✳ Text copyright © 2005 by Eileen Spinelli ✳ Illustrations copyright © 2005 by Kyrsten Brooker ✳ All rights reserved ✳ Designed by Jasmin Rubero ✳ Text set in Mrs. Eaves ✳ Manufactured in China on acid-free paper ✳ Library of Congress Cataloging-in-Publication Data ✳ Spinelli, Eileen. ✳ City angel / by Eileen Spinelli; illustrations by Kyrsten Brooker. ✳ p. cm. ✳ Summary: An angel spends her day watching over and taking care of the people and animals in a busy city. ✳ ISBN 0-8037-2821-2 ✳ [1. Guardian angels—Fiction. 2. Angels—Fiction. 3. City and town life—Fiction. 4. Kindness—Fiction. 5. Stories in rhyme.] I. Brooker, Kyrsten, ill. II. Title. ✳ PZ8.3.S759Ci 2005 ✳ [E]—dc21
2002011887

The art was created using collage and oil paint on gessoed watercolor paper.

For the Rosencrans family:
Andy and Emily, Anne, Sarah,
and John David

—E.S.

For Nicholas

—K.B.

City Angel starts her day
splashing high in fountain spray.
Dappling windows with some sun,
pigeon-flapping just for fun!

Next she makes a midtown stop
at the corner doughnut shop.
There she pets the kitchen cat
and, teasing—tweaks the baker's hat.

Among a stand of tires and weeds
City Angel plants some seeds
so a barren vacant lot
will become a garden plot.

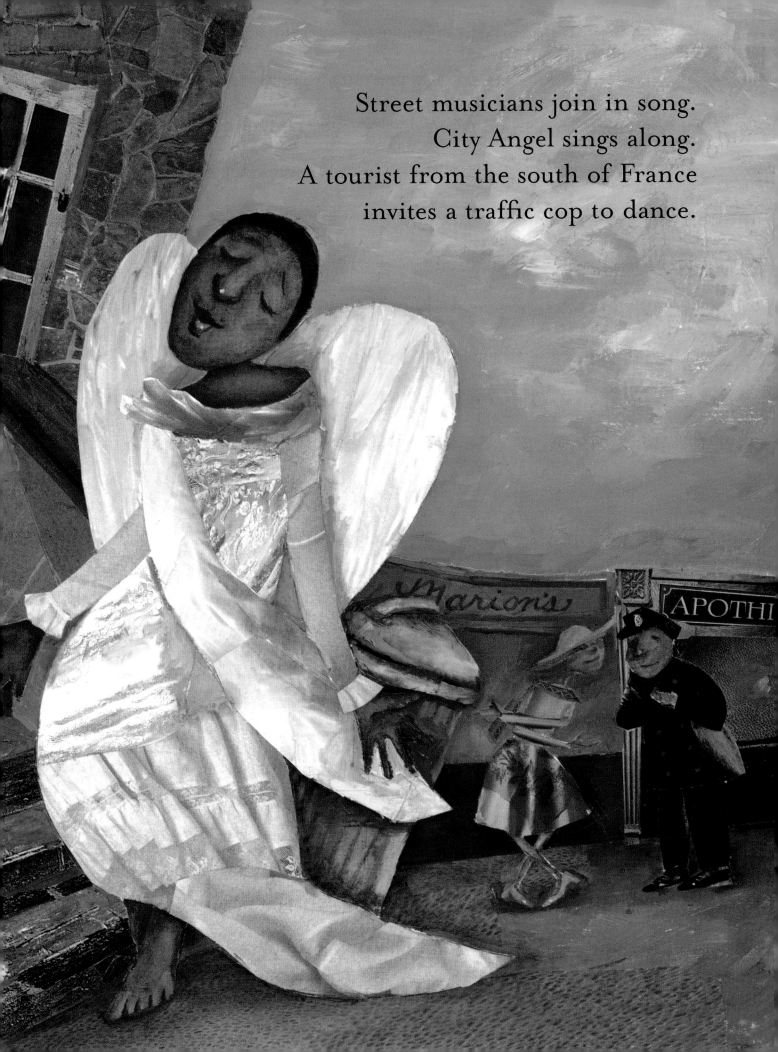

Street musicians join in song.
City Angel sings along.
A tourist from the south of France
invites a traffic cop to dance.

Skateboards cruising! Step aside!
City Angel hops a ride.
Pops an ollie. Whips a flip.
Airborne Angel—then—a dip!

Suddenly she hears a yelp.
Pet store owner needs some help.

Cranky child needs a lap.

Mayor needs a place to nap.

Firefighter, homeless man,
workers loading up a van,
window washer, nurse on call . . .
City Angel cares for all.

A lift . . .
   a smile . . .
      a soothing touch . . .
a laughing turn at double Dutch.

Lunch cart opens—gyro, steak . . .
City Angel takes a break.
Then off to give a welcome to
a newborn zebra at the zoo.

Horns are honking on the street.
Drivers grumpy from the heat.
Bully's dunking at the pool.
City Angel keeps things cool.

After school she grabs a broom,
tidies up a messy room,

gives the crossing guard a hug,

gently scolds
a litterbug.

B-ball player lets it fly.
Chain-link net's a mile high.
City Angel grants a wish:
Ball goes through the basket—swish!

Dusk falls softly, shadows flow.
One by one the streetlamps glow.
Bridges shimmer. Shops shut down.
Neon diner hums uptown.

City Angel soars above
the city she has come to love,
sprinkling dreams with twinkling light
long into the city night.